Gothic Bloom Horror Coloring Book:

A Dark Beauty Fantasy Coloring Realm

Unveil a world where shadows dance with the ethereal in Gothic Bloom Horror Adult Coloring Book: A Dark Beauty Fantasy Coloring Realm. Venture through enigmatic doorways into a domain where the eerie beauty of Gothic grandeur melds seamlessly with whimsical Fantasy. Each page invites you to breathe color into the Forsaken gardens, mysterious beings, and ancient, whispering ruins that hallmark this darkly enchanting realm. The solitary, high-quality pages ensure a premium coloring experience, allowing every hue to lay smooth and bold on the enduring pages. Whether a budding artist or a coloring connoisseur, Gothic Bloom invites you to a meditative journey through the quaint and mysterious, Forging a unique color saga that reflects the boundless realm of your imagination.

Let the shades of your creativity unveil the dark beauty awaiting each intricately designed page, inviting a solace and mystery only Found in the delicate balance between light and darkness. Within Gothic Bloom, every page is a doorway into the unknown, with only your colors to light the way through the mystic panes and wondrous gateways. Your journey through the hauntingly beautiful pages of Gothic Bloom is only bounded by the hues of your imagination. Let the colors flow, and the shadows dance as you unveil the enigmatic beauty in a world where Fantasy knows no bounds.

Coloring Tips & Tricks

Coloring can be a fun and relaxing hobby. Here are four tips and tricks to make the most out of your coloring experience:

1. ## Choose the Right Materials:
   - Coloring Tools: Depending on your coloring book's paper quality, choose suitable coloring tools. Colored pencils, gel pens, or fine markers are great for intricate designs, while crayons could work well for larger, bolder designs.

2. ## Techniques:
   - Layering: Start with a lighter hand and build up the color layers. This will give you more control over the color intensity and help in blending colors.
   - Shading: Adding shading can bring depth to your coloring. Use a darker shade of your base color to indicate shadows.

3. ## Color Theory:
   - Color Schemes: Choose colors that complement each other. Understanding basic color theory can help; for example, colors opposite each other on the color wheel are complementary.
   - Mood: Different colors evoke different moods. For instance, blues and greens are calming, while reds and oranges are energizing.

4. ## Practice Mindfulness:
   - Enjoy the Process: Rather than rushing to complete the page, take your time to enjoy the process of coloring. It's about the journey, not the destination.
   - Experiment: Don't be afraid to try new techniques or color combinations. Every page doesn't have to be a masterpiece; it's a chance to learn and grow your skills.

Lastly, always remember to sharpen your pencils for finer details and keep a spare piece of paper nearby to test your color combinations before applying them to your design.

Dear Valued Customer,

Thank you For purchasing our Adult Coloring Book "Gothic Bloom Horror Adult Coloring Book: A Dark Beauty Fantasy Coloring Realm." We hope it sparks joy and creativity in your day!

We'd greatly appreciate it if you could share your Feedback by leaving a review on our Amazon page. Feel Free to upload images of your colored pages as well—it's inspiring to see our designs brought to life through your creativity.

We look Forward to bringing you more imaginative adventures through our coloring books.

Warmest wishes and happy coloring,

- A. N. Scriptwell Publishing House

A.N. Scriptwell
Publishing House

Made in the USA
Las Vegas, NV
04 November 2023

80237391R00050